GIRAFFES IN THE SAVANNAH

A fairy tale about Harmony in Nature

Story by Gopal Dorai

Illustrations by Amanda Gordon Miller

Shooting Star Editions
American Literary Press

GIRAFFES IN THE SAVANNAH

Library of Congress
Cataloging in Publication Data
ISBN 978-1-934696-10-1

Published by

Shooting Star Editions
American Literary Press

8019 Belair Road, Suite 10
Baltimore, Maryland 21236
Manufactured in China

M any years ago, on the plains near the mighty Zambezi River in Africa, a herd of GIRAFFES gathered to eat and drink. The long drought had reduced the water level in the Zambezi to a mere trickle.

The animals had a hard time getting enough water to quench their thirst. Not only that, but most of the trees in the forest had lost their usual thick foliage during those long, dry, hot summer months. Constant grazing by the hungry, tall animals had almost completely stripped the trees of leaves, and the few leaves that still clung to the trees were dry and lifeless.

Even the tallest and strongest among the giraffe herd had trouble finding enough food to fill their huge stomachs. The animals were exhausted from their long search for food and water. At last they decided to ask the Tree God for a favor. The giraffes knew that the Tree God was kind and considerate. They thought that the trees existed for the welfare of their herd and other animals, and could not believe that their trees would go bare. Therefore they prayed long and hard to the Tree God for food to sustain them. They were sure that the Tree God would answer their prayers.

They knelt before the Tree God and said:

"Oh, Merciful God, please help us. We are your children. We are starving. We are dependent on you for our daily food. You know that we feed upon these tree branches every day. They are bare and dry, without many leaves. We cannot live without our favorite food. Please help us. The trees have not produced leaves on their limbs for so long. This drought is slowly killing all of us. You know we are hungry and starving. We need to eat. Please grow plenty of leaves on your branches. Let our children eat and survive. Have mercy on our pitiful souls."

The Tree God was pleased by their prayers. He really wanted to help them. So He thought to himself:

"Yes, the giraffes are right. The trees should produce leaves so that the animals can eat. But, alas, I am helpless too. The trees need moisture to grow leaves. This moisture comes from the rains. The rains have not visited our forests for so long. So I should ask the nearby Mountain God to help bring us rain. I need the help of the Mountain God."

He turned to the giraffe herd and told them: "Dear children, don't worry. I will see what I can do. You have to wait. I will come back to you soon to help you. Please rest for a while."

The giraffes were pleased and went to sleep.

The Tree God proceeded to the Mountain God and addressed him thus:

"Dear friend, I need your help desperately. My children, the giraffes, are starving for want of food. They need leaves on the tree branches so they can eat. Without rains, the trees are not producing any food for them. This is bad. We need rains right away. Please bring us some rains. Thank you for your help."

The Mountain God understood the plight of the animals. He really wanted to help them. But actually there was very little he could do to make rains. To bring about the rains, he needed the help and support of the Clouds. So he told the Tree God:

"Yes, dear friend, I understand. I wish I could help you. But without the cooperation of the Goddess of the Clouds, I cannot produce rains. The Goddess of the Clouds has not been visible around my head for months. If only the thick, moisture-laden Clouds would linger around me for a while, I could bring about all the rains we need. Then, not only could I feed the trees with plenty of water, but also fill the mighty Zambezi River. The water from the Clouds can help the whole of Mother Nature. When She smiles, all the creatures on the Savannah will benefit, I am sure."

The Tree God and the Mountain God now understood the importance of the Clouds. They realized that the Goddess of the Clouds was responsible for making rains around the world. Without rains, no one could really feed the trees as well as the mighty Zambezi River.

This was interesting. Yes, surely, without the help of the Goddess of the Clouds, neither the Tree God nor the Mountain God could help the giraffes. So, after some thinking, they decided to ask for help from the Goddess of the Clouds.

Together, they addressed the Goddess of the Clouds:

"Oh, sweet and rain-carrying Goddess of the Clouds, we need your help. Please hover around the Mountain so that you may blend with Him to produce rains in our forest. Our trees need moisture to grow leaves. Our children, the giraffes, need food and water for survival. Only you can help them survive. Please help us as fast as you can. We cannot wait."

Of course, the Goddess of the Clouds was very receptive to this urgent request. She really wanted to help all living creatures on Mother Earth. However, she needed the support of the Wind God to blow her toward the Mountain. Without help from the Wind God, she could not travel. Her speed and direction depended on the power of the great Wind God.

All the Gods and Goddesses depend on each other for help, just like human beings. So, together, the Tree God, the Mountain God and the Goddess of the Clouds asked the Wind God to help them.

They pleaded: "Oh, Great and powerful Wind God, the giraffes on the Savannah desperately need food and water. Their survival depends on the rains. The trees in the forest cannot grow leaves on their limbs without moisture. We pray that you should blow the Clouds in the direction of the Mountain to produce rains in the forest. All the children of Mother Earth look up to you for their survival. You alone can save us from ruin. You are powerful, as well as kind. Please help us all survive."

The combined prayers of the Tree God, the Mountain God and the Goddess of the Clouds had an impact on the Wind God. He decided to help them with all his might. But he was also realistic. He knew his own limitations and did not want to mislead his friends. He candidly told them thus:

"Yes, I can see how important my assistance is for the well being of Mother Nature and all her children. Yet I too have my own problem. I cannot promise to help you unless I get help from another source. And that source is the Sea Goddess. The Sea Goddess has to cooperate with me to push the moisture-laden Clouds toward the Mountain. So let us all together plead with the Sea Goddess to give us the moisture for the much needed rains."

This too was interesting. The Tree God, the Mountain God, the Goddess of the Clouds and the Wind God understood the key role of the Sea Goddess in making the much-needed rains. So they all went to her, knowing that without her assistance they were totally helpless!

Together, they said to her: "We know that the moisture-creating power of the Sea, blown by the Wind, creates Clouds which hover around the Mountain to produce rain. This rain feeds the forest and its thirsty trees. The trees need water to nourish them in order to produce leaves on their limbs. Mother Nature and all her children such as the giraffes need food and water to survive. Without your help, we cannot produce rain water. You play a key part in the great puzzle of Life. Please help us so that we can all work in harmony for our mutual survival."

The Sea Goddess understood the logic of their argument. She was willing to help. But there was one problem. She realized that the all-powerful Sun God was the source of all energy, light and heat in the whole world. It was the Sun's energy that heated up the Sea to create moisture-carrying Clouds. When the Sun smiled upon the Sea, its water evaporated to form Clouds laden with moisture.

Now the puzzle was at last resolved.

Together, the Tree God, the Mountain God, the Goddess of the Clouds, the Wind God, and the Sea Goddess worshipped the Sun. The Sun God was pleased.

He smiled on the Sea. She evaporated into moisture-carrying Clouds. The Wind swept the Clouds in the direction of the Mountain. When the Clouds hit his lofty summit, they cooled down to produce the life-giving rain.

The trees in the forest absorbed the rains through their system of roots. It nourished their branches and limbs to produce plenty of green leaves. The giraffes fed upon these leaves for their food. The mighty Zambezi River too was fed by the plentiful rain water falling on the forest floor. All the animals drank from the river to quench their thirst. They felt happy, content and restful.

The giraffes thanked the Tree God for his mercy and timely help. The Tree God then reminded them how he depended on all the other Elements in Nature: the Mountain God, the Goddess of the Clouds, the Wind God, the Sea Goddess and the Sun God. The giraffes were happy to learn about their mutual cooperation and combined efforts. They were grateful to all the Elements for all their hard work in making the leaves grow on the trees. And they happily feasted on the lush leaves growing on their favorite trees. When they were thirsty, they drank the cool waters of the mighty Zambezi River. And Mother Nature smiled on all the animals. They danced with joy, grateful for her bounty.

This story was written as a birthday present
for my granddaughter, Aarthi Ambrosi.